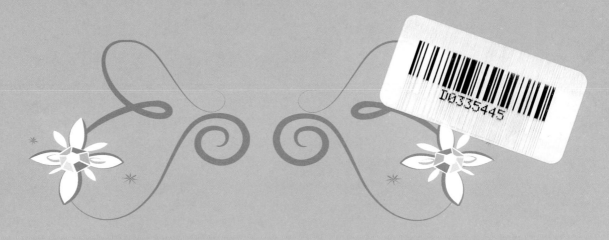

This book belongs to:

_____

Barbie™ AND THE MAGIC of PEGASUS

First published in Great Britain 2005
by Egmont UK Limited
239 Kensington High Street, London W8 6SA

ISBN 1 4052 2162 3

3 5 7 9 10 8 6 4 2

Printed in Singapore

BASED ON THE ORIGINAL SCREENPLAY BY

CLIFF RUBY & ELANA LESSER

Special thanks to Vicki Jaeger, Monica Lopez, Rob Hudnut, Shelley Dvi-Vardhana, Jesyca C. Durchin, Luke Carroll, Kelly Shin, Anita Lee, Sean Newton, Mike Douglas, Dave Gagnon, Derek Goodfellow, Teresa Johnston, and Walter P. Martishius.

Once upon a time, in a castle hidden away amid the tall, icy mountains, there lived a king and queen and their beautiful daughter, Annika. The king and queen worried about their daughter's safety, but they didn't know how brave the princess really was.

On the morning of Annika's sixteenth birthday, the queen rushed into her bedroom, excitedly. She was carrying a small gift box.

"Happy Birthday, Annika!" she cried. Then she stopped. "Annika?" The queen rang a bell, and in no time, servants were scurrying around the castle in a panic.

"The princess is missing! The princess is missing!"

Outside the castle, Princess Annika had no idea what trouble she had caused. She was celebrating her birthday by skating daringly along a frozen river bed. She jumped, spun in mid-air and twirled down to the ground, landing perfectly on one of her jewelled ice skates.

The princess didn't know she was being watched, until a ledge of snow collapsed, and a cute little polar bear came sliding towards her.

Annika named the bear cub Shiver, and decided to sneak her into the castle. But as she climbed the stairs, the princess heard a voice.

"Annika! Is that you?" cried the queen. Her parents rushed to her. "You're safe!"

"I was just skating," answered Annika. "Why do you always worry so much? Nothing's going to happen to me."

Just then, Shiver peeped out, and the princess scooped her up. "I met a friend," said Annika. The queen smiled and stepped forward to stroke Shiver.

"I'm sorry," the king interrupted, "but it is our job to keep you safe, and there's only one way to do that . . . no more skating."

Annika tried to argue, but she could see it was useless. Reluctantly, she handed over her skates and ran upstairs. "I hate you!" she cried, with tears in her eyes. Her parents looked at each other anxiously.

Up in her room that night, the sound of music drifted in through Annika's window. "Somebody's having fun on my birthday," she said. "Shiver, shall we go to a party?"

Annika quickly found her skates and they soon joined the party on the village pond.

Suddenly, a strange wind whistled through the trees and an eerie pink light coloured the sky. A huge griffin flew down onto the ice, and a hideous wizard climbed down from its back, pink light streaming from his wand.

The wizard walked up to Annika and smirked, "Allow me to introduce myself. I'm Wenlock . . . your future husband."

The king and queen had seen the strange light and rushed over at once. "Leave her alone," cried the king.

"Maybe you've forgotten what happened to your other daughter?" sneered the wizard. Annika was puzzled.

Then Wenlock asked her to marry him. "Of course not," she answered, horrified.

The wizard was so furious he turned the king, the queen and all the villagers into marble.

"Marry me and I'll set them free," sneered the wizard. "I'll give you three days before my spell becomes unbreakable!"

Before Annika could answer, a winged horse swept her to safety.

The horse flew up through the clouds to the Cloud Kingdom, where Annika met the beautiful Cloud Queen and her little princesses.

"We missed you, Brietta," cried Princess Rose. She turned to Annika and explained. "We've never had a real person here before, except for your sister, Brietta."

"My sister?" said Annika, confused. "But she's a horse . . ."

So the Cloud Queen told Annika her family's sad story. On Brietta's sixteenth birthday, Wenlock appeared and demanded to marry her. When Brietta refused, Wenlock turned her into a flying horse. The king and queen were devastated.

"Brietta couldn't bear to see them so unhappy," continued the Cloud Queen, "so she left and found refuge with us."

At last Annika understood her parents' anxiety. "I have to save them," she cried. "Can you help me?"

The Cloud Queen looked sad. "I have no powers over Wenlock."

"What about a Wand of Light?" asked Princess Rose. "That has the most powerful magic of all."

"It's built from a measure of courage, a ring of love, and a gem of ice lit by hope's eternal flame," explained the Cloud Queen.

Annika was determined to save her parents. "I'm going to build a Wand of Light, somehow," she said.

The Cloud Queen hung a crystal bell around Brietta's neck. "I wish I could do more to help you," she said. "Ring the bell if you need us."

Brietta carried Annika and Shiver to the deepest, darkest part of the forbidden forest. "The perfect place to find a measure of courage," Annika laughed, nervously.

The forest floor was covered with knotted tree roots and branches. Suddenly, Shiver tripped and tumbled helplessly into an icy gully.

Annika and Brietta rushed to find her, but they found themselves caught in a trap and left dangling, helplessly from the trees.

They heard a sound coming towards them and held their breath. Through the darkness, a horse appeared. Its handsome rider climbed down and freed them with a swish of his sword.

"My name is Aidan," he said.

But Annika was too worried about Shiver to talk to the handsome stranger. Without thinking, she slipped down into the gully, desperate to find her friend.

Down, down she tumbled, landing in an enormous pot, where she found a delighted Shiver. But when she looked up, she saw a huge, giant glaring at her menacingly.

"HMM, MORE LUNCH," boomed the giant. He was cutting up enormous vegetables and tossing them into the pot.

Annika pulled a long ribbon from her hair, and tried to use it to climb out of the pot with Shiver, but they kept getting knocked back.

Annika refused to give up. She called bravely to the giant, "The goliath down the road, he's a real giant. Big and strong. Compared to him, you're just a weakling."

The giant was furious, just as Annika had hoped. She realised that the giant was stupid and that she could escape by outwitting him. Clever Annika tricked the giant into chaining himself to a post. It was their chance to escape by climbing up the ribbon, and the giant was helpless to stop them! As Annika and Shiver ran, they met Aidan and Brietta coming to find them.

As Annika told the story of their escape, she held up the ribbon.

"It's your exact height and measure," said Brietta. "A measure of courage." The ribbon began to sparkle, then it turned to solid silver.

"A staff," cried Annika, "for the Wand of Light!"

Just as Aidan was turning to leave, Annika noticed his sword.

"I made it myself," said Aidan.

Annika was amazed. "When we have the three parts of the Wand, we'll need somebody like you to put them together," she said.

The four friends travelled on through the night until they arrived at a miserable shack. A shady gem dealer, called Ferris, lived inside.

Annika told him that they were looking for a gem of ice lit by hope's eternal flame. Ferris gave her an old map that might help them in return for Annika's jewelled skates.

They trudged through the snow for some time before they realised that the map was a fake! Reluctantly, they stopped for the night.

The next morning, Annika and Aidan watched, amazed, as beams of sunlight sparkled on the glacier ahead.

"The gem is somewhere on top of that glacier!" cried Annika.

Brietta carried them over the glacier and across a set of sparkling stepping stones to a message carved in the ice. It was written in runes, but Aidan understood them.

"Take only what you need, but never from greed," he read.

Suddenly, the ground rumbled beneath them and a secret passage opened up. Inside was a maze of tunnels. They followed a light to a huge cavern, where sunbeams shone in through a hole in the roof. Hundreds of diamonds glistened like stars before them. Annika reached to take one, and the ground rumbled gently beneath her. Aidan pulled a diamond from the wall, and the cavern rumbled again.

"You can't be greedy," Annika reminded him.

"I know," said Aidan.

But Shiver was not so careful. She was busy collecting gems and didn't notice the cavern collapsing around her. Annika quickly snatched her up, and Brietta carried them to safety through the maze of icy tunnels.

As Annika held the staff and the diamond, they started to glow. "Look at them!" she cried. "Now all we need is the ring of love."

Aidan hesitated. "Maybe I could forge one?" he suggested, shyly.

"Why didn't the cavern collapse when you picked the diamond?" she asked, curiously. "It wasn't greed. So why do you need a diamond?"

Aidan told Annika how he had once been very foolish. "My parents trusted me with all their savings, and I lost the money at cards. Maybe if I pay them back, they'll see me again."

Now there was just one thing missing for them to complete the Wand of Light: Aidan needed metal to make the ring. Just then, Brietta dropped her crown at Aidan's feet.

"The ring of love!" gasped Annika. "Nobody said the ring had to be for your finger."

With the heat of the fire, Aidan forged the staff and crown together. He fixed the diamond in the crown. The Wand of Light was beautiful.

Annika lifted the Wand and whispered a wish. A cloud of sparkling, magic dust surrounded Brietta. When it disappeared, the horse had gone, and Brietta was a beautiful girl of sixteen, once again.

But there was just one problem. Brietta couldn't fly any more . . .

Brietta rang her crystal bell, and soon two beautiful winged horses swooped down to help them. The Cloud Queen had kept her promise.

As Annika turned to say goodbye to Aidan, she gazed at the Wand of Light. "We wouldn't have this without you," she said, gratefully.

The sisters soared through the sky, but their happiness was not to last. Suddenly, Wenlock and his griffin appeared in front of them.

"Strike her," cried Wenlock, firing his mighty wand at Brietta, and sending her tumbling into the snow,.

Annika was furious. She pointed the Wand of Light at Wenlock. "Destroy him!" she cried. But nothing happened. Instead, Wenlock flashed his wand at Annika, and the Wand of Light flew to him.

With another flash of his wand, Wenlock split the ice beneath Annika's feet and she slipped deep into the snow.

Just as Shiver and Brietta began their search for Annika, Aidan returned. He found Annika and lifted her gently from the snow.

Aidan took Annika to the Cloud Palace to recover. After a few days' rest, she was soon herself again. "I need to get the Wand of Light before sunset," she said when she awoke.

Brietta led Annika and Aidan to a secret ice tunnel. They pulled on some skates and were soon gliding through it. Aidan could skate just as well as Annika!

The tunnel led them straight into Wenlock's palace. Inside, they saw Wenlock banging the Wand of Light to try to make it work. When nothing happened, he threw it away in disgust.

Annika searched quietly for the Wand while Aidan fought off the evil griffin. As she picked the Wand up, the diamond fell out. But Aidan rushed to give her his own precious diamond. He was prepared to give it up for the love of Annika.

Now Annika understood how to use the Wand of Light. Pointing it at Wenlock, she spoke without anger, "For the love of my family and my people, I ask you to break all of Wenlock's spells."

Wenlock's wand exploded into fiery pieces, his griffin turned back into a scrawny cat, and Wenlock shrank into the miserable troll he really was.

The spell was broken! Just before sunset, the king, the queen
and all the villagers started to move once more.

The next day, Annika hugged her parents. "Are you ready for
a surprise?" she smiled. The king and queen gasped in amazement,
as their lost daughter, Brietta, walked into the room.

Later that same day, Aidan approached his father nervously.
"Aidan, oh Aidan!" his father cried. "I hoped I'd see you again."
"I lost hope . . . until . . ." said Aidan, stretching his hand out to
Annika. "Father, there's someone I'd like you to meet."

High up in the Cloud Palace, Brietta gave the Cloud Queen the Wand of Light. "Will you keep this safe, your highness?" she asked.

The Cloud Queen accepted the Wand. "I'd be honoured. It will be the first star in the sky every night . . . and a reflection of their love," she said.

And through the Palace window, she and Brietta looked down to a couple skating gracefully on a magical cloud beneath them.

Annika leaped into the air and Aidan caught her. As he lowered her gently onto the ice, Aidan twirled Annika close, and they gazed at each other, lovingly.

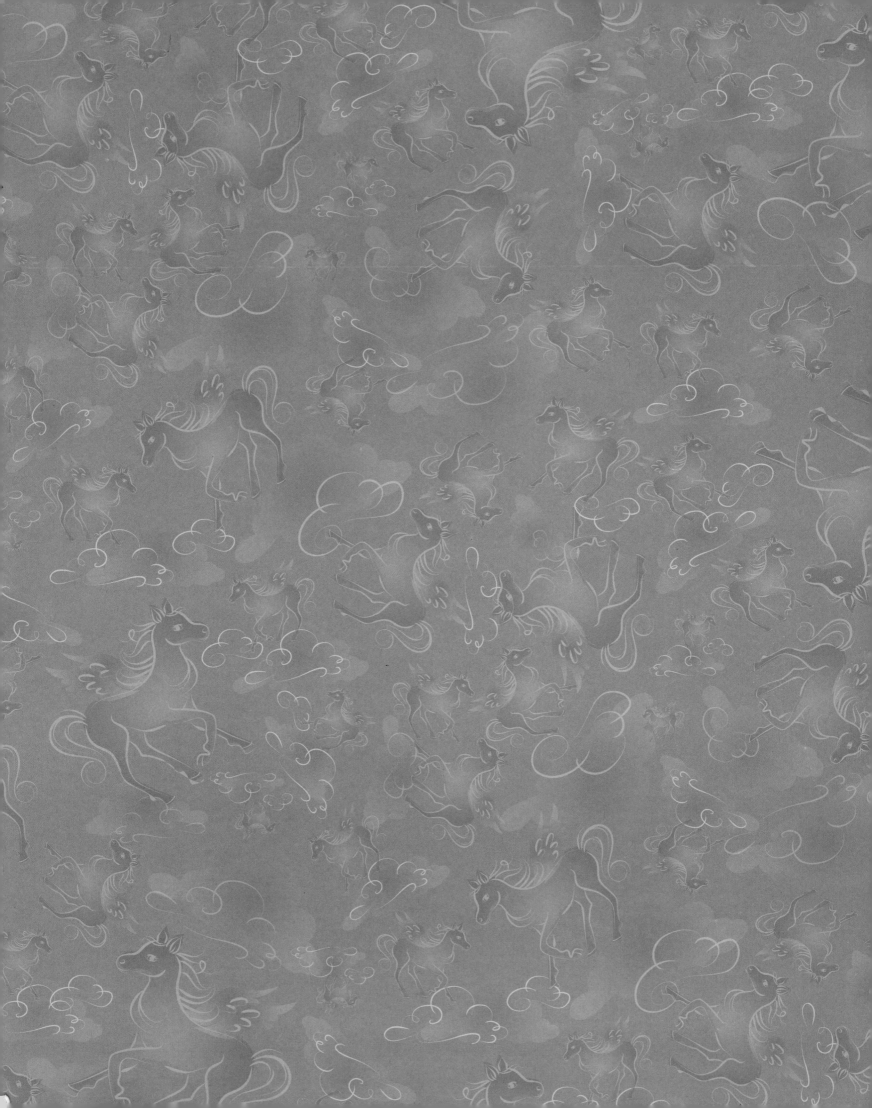